Ready, Set, Goal!

★ Also by ★
Debbie Dadey

MERMAID TALES

Coming Soon

Mermaid Tales

★ Debbie Dadey ★

Illustrated by
Tatevik Avakyan

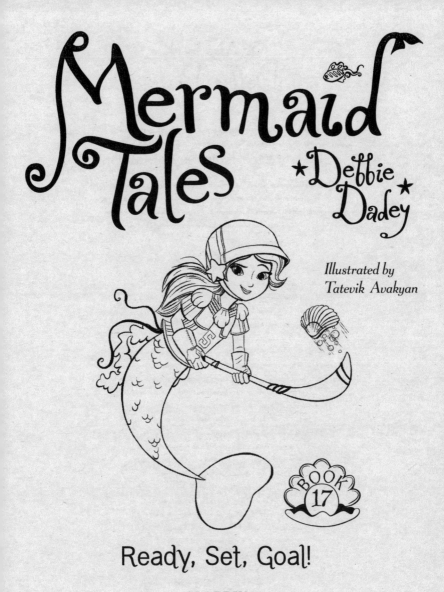

BOOK 17

Ready, Set, Goal!

ALADDIN

NEW YORK   LONDON   TORONTO   SYDNEY   NEW DELHI

ALADDIN

An imprint of Simon & Schuster Children's Publishing Division

1230 Avenue of the Americas, New York, NY 10020

First Aladdin paperback edition September 2017

Text copyright © 2017 by Debbie Dadey

Illustrations copyright © 2017 by Tatevik Avakyan

Also available in an Aladdin hardcover edition.

All rights reserved, including the right of reproduction in whole or in part in any form.

ALADDIN and related logo are registered trademarks of Simon & Schuster, Inc.

For information about special discounts for bulk purchases,

please contact Simon & Schuster Special Sales at 1-866-506-1949

or business@simonandschuster.com.

The Simon & Schuster Speakers Bureau can bring authors to your live event.

For more information or to book an event contact the

Simon & Schuster Speakers Bureau at 1-866-248-3049

or visit our website at www.simonspeakers.com.

Series designed by Karin Paprocki

Cover designed by Nina Simoneaux

The text of this book was set in Belucian Book.

Manufactured in the United States of America 0819 OFF

2 4 6 8 10 9 7 5 3

Library of Congress Control Number 2016962154

ISBN 978-1-4814-8709-2 (hc)

ISBN 978-1-4814-8708-5 (pbk)

ISBN 978-1-4814-8710-8 (eBook)

For Brian Johnson—

so happy to have you in our family

* * * *

Acknowledgments

Thanks to all the great encouragement from Ara, Ellison, Chloe, Nola, Sophie, Ashlyn, Marisa, and all my wonderful readers.

Contents

1

Tiger Sharks Score!

SHELLY SIREN SWUNG HER whalebone stick with all her might. She held her breath as she smacked the shell and it soared through the water. Poseidon Prep's octopus goalie spread out his eight tentacles to stop her from scoring.

A split mersecond later, the shell whizzed through a tiny space between the octopus's arms and slammed into the treasure chest behind him.

Shelly's friend Echo Reef screamed from the sidelines, "Goal!" just as the announcer bellowed, "Trident Academy scores!"

★ 2 ★

Shelly let out a sigh of relief.

"The Trident Academy Tiger Sharks win!" yelled the referee.

Echo and the Tail Flippers gymnastics squad flipped around and around on the side of the kelp field. The entire crowd from Shelly's school, Trident Academy, roared in excitement. Her teammates lifted her up on their shoulders. Rocky Ridge cheered, "Go Shelly!"

Shelly felt embarrassed. She usually didn't like attention. But she was filled with excitement when Coach Barnacle swam over and told them some exciting news.

"Congrats, team! We're going to the Shell Wars Championships!"

★ 3 ★

"Sweet seaweed!" Shelly said. The Shell Wars Championships were the biggest games in the entire ocean. Teams from all over competed for the Golden Trophy. Not only that, but the matches were held in the faraway glittering city of Atlantis. Shelly had heard it was the most fin-tastic place ever, filled with fascinating human objects.

Rocky's father, Mayor Ridge, swam up to a podium on the field and announced, "Congratulations, Trident Academy! In commemoration of this wonderful turn of events, I declare tomorrow Trident City Shell Wars Day. Every merperson will get the morning off from work and school. We'll have a parade in front of the Trident City Plaza Hotel to honor all the team members of the Trident Academy Tiger Sharks."

Echo and the rest of her gymnastics group gathered beside the Shell Wars team. One of the Tail Flippers, Pearl Swamp, tapped Mayor Ridge on the shoulder. "Mayor, can the Tail Flippers be part of the parade?"

"Of course!" Mayor Ridge said with a smile. "These championship games will be the biggest thing to ever happen to Trident City in my lifetime. A Trident Academy team hasn't gone in over a hundred years! Let the celebration begin!"

2

Parade

EVERYONE IN TRIDENT CITY is here for the championship parade," Shelly told her team-mates. She was perched on the flat back of an enormous manta ray as it floated slowly down the street. Shelly's teammates were scattered around the ray's back. They all waved at the huge crowd. After the parade, the Trident Academy Shell Wars team and the Tail Flippers would be off to Atlantis.

"Hooray for Trident Academy!" yelled a merlady named Lillian. "You are mervelous!" Lillian was the new bride of Mr. Fangtooth, their school's cafeteria worker. Mr. Fangtooth, who was usually very grumpy, actually smiled as the ray passed by them.

Shelly pushed her long red hair out of her face and waved to the crowd. She stopped smiling when she spotted her grandfather. He wouldn't be going to Atlantis with the team, and Shelly would miss him. For as long as she could remember, it had been

just the two of them living in their small apartment above Trident City's People Museum. Shelly had left him only once before, when she and her merbuddies had visited Neptune's Castle.

"Have fun, Shelly!" Grandfather yelled.

Now Shelly had to grin. She knew her grandfather would be cheering her on from Trident City. Behind the manta ray, the Trident Academy Pep Band blasted out a lively tune.

When the parade was over, Mayor Ridge made a speech congratulating the team again. Then it was time to leave! After saying good-bye to their families, the team and the Tail Flippers, along with Coach Barnacle and Assistant Coach Sarah

SeaLion, stayed on the huge manta ray, which would sail through the ocean to Atlantis.

The water grew colder as the ray left Trident City behind. Everyone onboard scrambled to find a comfortable seat for the long trip. Luckily, Shelly's two best friends had saved her a soft sponge. They waved her over.

"That was one shell-tacular parade," Kiki Coral said as Shelly plopped down beside her.

"I'm so glad you became the team manager," Shelly told Kiki. "This trip wouldn't be as fun without you and the Tail Flippers."

Earlier in the school year, Kiki had volunteered to manage the Shell Wars team.

That meant she had to keep track of all the equipment. She was also in charge of making sure that every team member knew about the game schedules. It was a very important job, but Kiki was up for the challenge!

"What do you mean there are no snacks?" someone complained from the front of the ray. Shelly turned to see Pearl with her hands on her hips and a frown on her face.

"Pearl!" Kiki called. "Come here! I brought snacks." Kiki opened a small crate filled with goodies.

"Yum!" Shelly said. "Cuttlefish candy!"

"Help yourself," Kiki told her. "My mother sent these to me." Kiki's family lived far away in the Eastern Oceans, and her parents often sent treats from home.

★ 11 ★

Pearl squeezed onto the sponge seat beside Shelly and sniffed. "Thanks. If I'd known they were going to starve us, I would have brought my own," she muttered, grabbing a handful of candy.

After munching on snacks, the mergirls sang "Shark, the sharpnose sevengill" until their voices were hoarse and Coach Barnacle yelled for them to get some rest. Shelly tried to nap, but her eyes just wouldn't close.

After many hours of traveling, Shelly glimpsed the city of Atlantis in the distance. The tall, shiny buildings gleamed and sparkled in the water.

Shelly shook Echo awake before pointing ahead. "There it is!"

"Wow! It's just as beautiful as the stories say." Kiki sat up and rubbed her eyes. "Did you know that Atlantis used to be a human city? It sank to the bottom of the ocean many years ago."

"I know!" Echo squealed and wiggled her pink tail. "I can't wait to explore it." She loved anything that had to do with people.

The manta ray pulled up beside a sprawling stone building with a sign that read BEST OCEAN HOTEL. Hundreds of merkids were practicing their Shell Wars moves in front of the hotel. One group worked on tossing a shell into a treasure chest while another threw shells back and forth. Not one of them missed a shot!

"Whoa!" Rocky said from the back of the

ray. "Those players are splashing good!"

Shelly gulped. Every player looked fin-tastic! It was hard to believe that Trident Academy would be playing against them tomorrow.

Pearl stared at the other players with her pointy nose held high. "They're okay, but they can't touch our team. Go Trident Academy Tiger Sharks!"

Shelly smiled. Still, she didn't take her eyes off the other teams. What would it take to win the championship games? Would her team be able to swim as fast? Pass the shell as quickly? Shelly liked to think she was a good player, but was she good enough?

3

End of the Ocean

EVERYONE OFF THE RAY!" Coach Barnacle bellowed. "Coach Sarah will hand out your room assignments. Kiki will pass out the schedules. Go straight to your rooms, unpack, and then meet back here in exactly thirty merminutes. Coach

Sarah will be taking you on a tour of Atlantis while I attend a meeting with the other coaches. After that, the team will gather back here for a quick practice. Then tonight we will all attend the official Shell Wars banquet at the Aqua-Dome next door."

The ray swayed as everyone leaped off their sponge seats and floated toward the hotel doors. With all the pushing and shoving of her teammates, Shelly lost track of Echo and Kiki. Outside the hotel, Shelly took her room key from Coach Sarah. "You're in number fifteen," Coach Barnacle's assistant told her. "You'll be sharing with a few other mergirls."

Inside, the hotel's bright-blue walls were

lined with red doors, each with a number on it. Shelly found room number fifteen and pushed open the heavy door.

"Pearl!" Shelly said.

"Oh!" Pearl said. "If I'd known my room was going to be so ordinary, I would have stayed home."

Shelly sighed. It was just her luck to share a room with the most spoiled mergirl in Trident City. She looked around. Two sponge beds were covered with red kelp blankets. Big scallop shells and cockle-shells decorated the walls. "It looks totally wavy to me," she said, dropping her bag next to one of the beds.

"Hey! That's my bed," Pearl said.

"Fine." Shelly immediately pushed her

belongings over to the other sponge. "It doesn't matter to me."

Then the door swung open wide. "Thank Neptune! We found it," Echo said.

"Hi," Kiki said with a wave. "We went to room fifty-one by mistake."

Pearl's eyes got really wide. "For shark's sake! Do you mean I have to share this tiny room with three other mergirls? And share a sponge bed?"

Shelly looked at Echo and tried not to laugh.

"Like it or not," Kiki said. "We don't have much time. We have to meet out front in just a few merminutes. I'll share a sponge with you, Pearl. I'm the smallest and I don't take up much space."

★ 18 ★

Pearl rolled her eyes, but didn't say anything else.

"Come on," Echo urged them. "Let's
go. Coach Sarah is taking us on a tour of
Atlantis. I can't wait!"

4

Flag Fish

THEIR TOUR GUIDE, LESLIE Levee, waved a flag fish and motioned for the Trident Academy group to follow her across a black rock bridge. "The city of Atlantis was built by Poseidon," she informed them, "for his son Atlas."

"Who is Posy Den?" Rocky asked.

"It's pronounced Po-si-don," Kiki explained. "It's the Greek name for Neptune, the original king of the sea."

"What is a Greek?" Rocky asked. Then he shook his head. "Never mind, I really don't care. Anyway, check that out!"

All the merkids looked toward a huge white-marble building with pillars of gleaming gold. Its enormous doors opened wide beneath a carving of the first sea god. "I'd like to live there," Pearl said.

"I don't think that's someone's house," Kiki said. "I think that's a—"

Leslie Levee waved her flag fish at Kiki. "Float along now! We have lots to see."

Kiki's face turned red as the tour guide led them forward. "This city was built in circles," Leslie explained. "We just left the outer circle by crossing over the first of three main bridges that protected the Temple of Poseidon from invasion. Of course, attacking armies aren't what caused Atlantis to sink."

"What did cause it to sink?" Shelly asked, very curious.

Leslie Levee shook her head. "No one knows for sure, but most merfolk suspect it had to do with the volcano." Leslie pointed into the distance, where Shelly could see steam rising from a large vent.

Pearl must have seen it too, because she asked in a worried voice, "It's not going to erupt while we're here, is it?"

"No, Atlantis sank over three thousand years ago. I think we're pretty safe," Leslie Levee said with a little smile.

Still, Pearl gulped. "I hope you're right."

"Now, without further interruption, we'll move over the red bridge and through the city's residential area, where most of Atlantis's merfolk live. Then we'll tour the temple." Leslie Levee pointed to the marble-and-gold building on the hill.

Pearl groaned. "So it's not a house. Boring!"

Echo gasped. "Oh no! If that's Poseidon's temple, we can't go inside!"

"Why not?" Shelly asked. She was surprised that Echo didn't want to visit a building that was made by humans.

Echo's dark eyes were wide as she whispered, "Don't you know about the curse?"

The Curse of Atlas

WHAT CURSE?" SHELLY asked as they floated over the red stone bridge. Echo shuddered. "I can't even say it, it's so terrible."

"It's just a legend," Kiki explained. "Some merfolk believe that if you see a spookfish while you're inside the temple, you'll be cursed by Atlas."

"And what is the Curse of Atlas?" Pearl asked.

"I'm not sure," Kiki admitted.

"I know," Rocky blurted out, squeezing between Shelly and Pearl. "It means that rotten, horrible, awful things will happen to you!" He wiggled his fingers above his head in a creepy way.

"Don't be silly!" Pearl snapped at Rocky.

"There's no wavy way I'm going in there," Echo said firmly, crossing her arms. "I don't want rotten, horrible, awful things to happen to me."

"Echo's afraid of a little bitty fish," Rocky teased.

"Spookfish are pretty rare anyway. I've never seen one in my whole life," Kiki told Echo.

Shelly agreed with Kiki. "I've only seen pictures of them. Besides, that curse is just an old story. There's nothing to worry about."

But Echo stopped short when they came to a wide white bridge with statues carved into the stone.

"This is called Kleite's Bridge," Leslie Levee announced. "Next, we'll be entering Poseidon's temple. The building is thousands of years old, so please look but don't touch anything inside."

Echo shook her head. "I'm not going."

"But you love human objects!" Kiki exclaimed.

Echo wrapped her pink tail around a nearby statue and refused to swim forward.

"We can't just leave you alone in a strange city," Shelly whispered. "Coach Sarah told us to stick with the group."

Leslie Levee waved her flag fish at Echo and asked, "Is something wrong?"

"Yes," Echo said at the same time that Pearl said "No."

"We're coming," Shelly said. Then in a low voice, she told Echo, "Just close your eyes, and I'll pull you along."

Echo nodded, squeezed her eyes shut, and let Shelly tug her across the bridge and through the temple's doors.

"Oh, it's so beautiful!" Pearl squealed once they were inside.

Echo whimpered. Shelly could tell Echo wanted to see, so Shelly described everything to her merfriend. "This huge room is filled with even more pillars of gold, and the ceiling has a carved ivory picture of Poseidon with gold, silver, and copper fish all around him. The walls are made of polished silver that look like waves of water."

"I've never seen anything like it," Kiki whispered.

"It's even prettier than the front hall of Trident Academy," Pearl admitted.

"Tell me more!" Echo cried.

Just then Shelly glanced past her friends through an open doorway and gasped. She couldn't believe what she saw!

"What's wrong?" Echo asked.

"Nothing," Shelly said quickly.

But something was wrong. Very wrong.

6

Spookfish

SHELLY CLOSED HER EYES tight. When she opened them, what she had seen was gone. But it had been there! The dreaded spookfish had stared right at her with its strange barrel-shaped eyes before slithering away. It had happened so fast. Shelly looked around. Had she been the only one to see it? No one else seemed upset, but Shelly sure was.

"And now, students," Leslie Levee said, "we'll be floating down one of the temple's main hallways. You'll see engravings of Poseidon and his family in the copper walls."

The whole group swam forward, except for Echo and Shelly. Echo still had her eyes closed. "Aren't we supposed to be moving?" she asked Shelly.

When Shelly didn't respond, Echo asked, "Shelly! Are you all right?"

Shelly gulped. She knew she was being silly. After all, the curse was just an old made-up legend. Wasn't it?

She towed Echo down the hallway and bumped right into Kiki. "Oops, sorry," Shelly whispered.

Kiki took one glance at Shelly and asked softly, "Are you ill? You look like you're ready to throw up."

Rocky, who was floating nearby, pushed away from Shelly and hollered, "Don't puke on me!"

Leslie Levee jerked around with a stern look on her face. "There will be no throwing up in the temple! Coach SeaLion, please take that student outside."

Coach Sarah SeaLion swiftly guided Shelly toward the entrance, leaving Kiki to lead Echo.

Once she was outside, Shelly closed

her eyes. She really did feel sick. Was it because of the curse? Through the temple's open doors she could hear Leslie Levee telling the students about Poseidon's son Atlas. "Because he revolted against the Olympians," she explained, "Atlas was forced to carry the heavens upon his shoulders for the rest of his life. This is an engraving of that story."

Shelly shuddered. Was that what would happen to her because she'd seen the dreaded spookfish? Or would it be something worse? What had Rocky said? *Rotten, horrible, awful things will happen to you!*

Shelly and Coach Sarah sat on a long marble bench near the temple's entrance.

"Do you need to see a doctor?" Coach Sarah asked.

Shelly shook her head. What was bothering her couldn't be fixed by a doctor. She tried to concentrate on the beautiful vase sitting on a stone table beside them. It was filled with red passion flowers. The color soothed Shelly.

After a long wait, the rest of the group joined them outside. Kiki, Echo, and Pearl swam up to Shelly.

"Are you all right?" Kiki asked.

Shelly didn't want her friends to be worried, so she

smiled. "I'm fine! It must have been a touch of decompression sickness."

"That makes sense! Atlantis is deeper in the ocean than Trident City, which can make you ill," Pearl told them. "My father warned me about it. He said the best thing to do is drink plenty of kelp juice."

Shelly nodded. "I'll do that when we get back to the hotel."

"Is it safe to open my eyes now?" Echo asked.

"Yes, we're outside," Kiki said, and Echo popped open her eyes.

Pearl sniffed. "I can't believe you kept your eyes closed the whole time we were in the temple. You missed all the good stuff."

"Well, I didn't want to be cursed," Echo told her.

Pearl shook her head and her blond hair floated around her face. "That curse is silly. I bet someone in Atlantis made it up to make their city seem mysterious."

Shelly smiled. Without meaning to, Pearl had made Shelly feel much, much better.

"What could be more mysterious than a human city that sank into the ocean?" Kiki asked.

"All right, merstudents," Coach Sarah said. "It's time to head back to the hotel. The Tiger Sharks have practice in twenty merminutes."

But as Shelly hopped up from the marble

bench, her blue tail whacked the vase next to her. She watched in horror as it toppled over and crashed to the ground. Passion flowers scattered everywhere as the vase shattered into hundreds of pieces.

"Your school will have to pay for that," Leslie Levee said, looking at the damage and shaking her head. "Luckily, it's not an antique."

Shelly didn't feel lucky. In fact, she felt cursed!

7

Bubbles

SHELLY COULDN'T SEEM TO DO anything right at Shell Wars practice. First, she accidently slapped Rocky on the nose with the end of her whalebone stick. Then, every time she was supposed to pass the shell to

Adam Pelagic she tossed it too hard and it soared off the kelp field.

Rocky tapped her on the shoulder. "In case you've forgotten, the point of Shell Wars is to get the shell into the treasure chest, not to knock out your teammates!"

Shelly felt her face turning red. She nodded and looked at the octopus guarding their treasure chest. Usually she was pretty good at sneaking the shell into the chest to score, but today she could only think about the curse.

Just a few merminutes later, her shell flew onto the wrong playing field and gave the Thonis City team's octopus goalie a black eye. Half the Thonis team yelled at her and the other half gave her dirty looks. "I'm so sorry!" Shelly wailed to the octopus.

Things didn't get any better when Shelly opened the door to her hotel room and slammed into Pearl's tail. "Ouch!" Pearl shrieked. "Are you trying to twist my fin?"

"I apologize," Shelly said. "I'm having a terrible day!"

Echo put her arm around Shelly. "You're probably just worried about the games tomorrow. Why don't you take a nice long bath to relax?"

Shelly didn't usually like baths, but maybe one would make her feel better. She went into the bathroom and turned on the warm water in the big shell tub. "Here are some bubbles to make you feel better." Kiki drizzled in a tiny bit of sweet-smelling liquid as the warm water replaced the cold ocean-floor water. While the tub filled, Shelly went to get some clean clothes from her bag.

"Look at this," Kiki said, coming out of the bathroom and holding up the schedule for the championship games. "The Rays are going to perform during halftime at the final game!"

"That's tail-kicking!" Echo said. The Rays are a cute merboy band that the girls love.

"Oooh, I adore the Rays," Pearl said. "I'd better make sure I brought my Venus comb." She disappeared into the bathroom.

Suddenly the mergirls heard a scream. A huge wall of bubbles roared out of the bathroom, carrying Pearl on top. "Save me!" she squealed.

It took the mergirls an hour and every kelp towel they had, but they finally wiped up all the bubbles. "I don't know how that happened," Kiki said.

"I only put a little bit of bubbles in the tub."

"I snuck in and poured in half the bottle," Echo admitted. "But I wanted Shelly to really enjoy it!"

"Neither of you is to blame!" Shelly said miserably. "It was my fault."

"But you didn't add any bubbles," Kiki said.

"No," Shelly said, shaking her head, "but I'm the one with the curse."

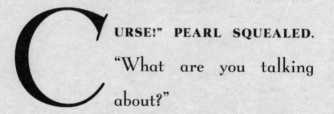

Curse Trouble

CURSE!" PEARL SQUEALED. "What are you talking about?"

Echo fell back on the sponge bed and whispered, "Oh no! Don't tell me you saw a spookfish at the temple!"

Big tears filled Shelly's eyes. She was so

upset, she couldn't even speak. Finally she managed a nod.

"Oh, Shelly." Kiki patted her arm. "I'm sure the curse isn't real."

Pearl slapped her tail on the floor, causing a leftover bubble to pop. "It isn't real. It's just a silly story."

"Then how do you explain all the horrible things that have happened to me? I broke that vase at the temple. I hurt Rocky! I whacked a goalie in the eye!"

"Yeah, but Shell Wars players often get hit during a game," Kiki told them.

"But the goalie wasn't even on our practice field," Shelly explained. "My shell soared two fields away. That couldn't have happened on its own!"

Pearl shrugged. "Maybe it was just a weird accident."

"But what about your tail?" Shelly asked Pearl. "And then all the bubbles?"

Pearl twisted her long strand of pearls and nodded. "Yeah. It sounds like you're cursed, all right."

"Pearl! How could you say that?" Kiki said.

Echo frowned at Pearl. "I thought you didn't even believe in the curse."

Pearl shrugged. "That was before all those terrible things happened to Shelly."

Shelly sank down onto the bed beside Echo. "What am I going to do? I'll ruin our team's chances of winning the Shell Wars Championship!"

"It's not your fault," Echo told Shelly.

"There has to be something we can do," Kiki said.

"There is," Pearl said with a smile. "It's a good thing I'm here!"

9

Pearl's Cure

YOU KNOW HOW TO BREAK A curse?" Kiki asked Pearl.

Pearl nodded. "I read all about it in a recent issue of MerStyle magazine," she told them.

"I don't remember seeing that," Echo said, "and I've read every one."

"It was a special issue," Pearl said matter-of-factly. "My father picked it up for me when he was in New Ocean City." New Ocean City was known as the fashion capital of the sea, so it made sense that there would be special magazines there.

"What did it say?" Shelly asked. "Is it hard to break a curse?"

Pearl frowned. "It won't be easy, but if we all work together, we can do it before tonight's banquet."

Shelly gave Pearl a hug. "Thank you! What's first?"

Pearl twisted her pearl necklace and said, "Let me think. Oh yes, first we need a horseshoe crab."

"I saw some at a market near the hotel," Kiki said. "I could swim over and get one!"

"Wave-tastic!" Pearl said. "Then we'll need a shark's tooth."

"Where in the ocean are we going to get a shark's tooth?" Echo asked. "I'm pretty sure a shark won't just give us one without a fight."

"Rocky has one!" Shelly said. "He found it a long time ago, and sometimes he wears it around his neck for good luck. Maybe he'll let us borrow it."

"I'll ask him," Echo told her merfriends.

"Anything else?" Shelly asked Pearl.

"Yes, we need something sweaty and stinky that you've worn recently, sea bamboo, and a triangular butterflyfish," Pearl

★ 52 ★

said as if she was checking off a list of things in her mind.

Kiki picked up the team schedule. "It says right here that butterflyfish will be served at tonight's banquet dinner. I'll get some from the kitchen."

"Fin-tastic!" Shelly said. "And I have my sweaty shirt from today's practice. All we need is some sea bamboo and we're set."

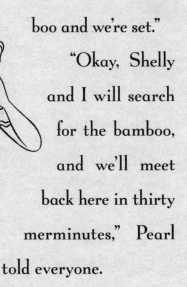

"Okay, Shelly and I will search for the bamboo, and we'll meet back here in thirty merminutes," Pearl told everyone.

"And then we'll break the curse?" Echo asked hopefully.

Pearl nodded. Shelly crossed her fins. Operation Reverse the Curse was on!

Reverse the Curse

WE DID IT!" ECHO SAID. An hour later, everything they needed to break the curse was spread out on a sponge bed in their hotel room.

Shelly nodded. "We searched all over Atlantis for the sea bamboo."

"I had to tell the cook a fib in order to get the butterflyfish. I said that one of our team members wasn't feeling well," Kiki said.

"That wasn't a lie," Shelly reminded her. "Ever since I saw the spookfish, I've felt terrible!"

"Rocky made me promise to give his shark's tooth back before tomorrow's game," Echo said. "It wasn't easy getting him to let me borrow it."

"You can return it at the banquet tonight," Pearl said. "Now we have to take all these things to the temple."

"The temple!" Shelly squealed. "That's where the trouble began."

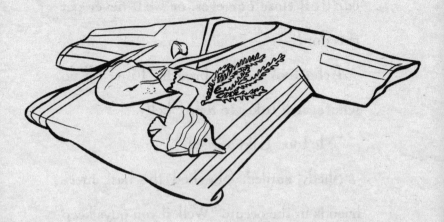

Pearl nodded her head before wrapping the fish, crab, bamboo, and shark's tooth inside Shelly's sweaty shirt. "Exactly, but don't worry. Even if we see the spookfish again, the cure will be with us."

"Well, I'm going to close my eyes again, just in case," Echo said.

"Me too!" Shelly and Kiki said together.

Pearl put her hands on her hips. "We

can't all close our eyes, or we'll never get this done!"

Echo took a deep breath. "Fine. I'll do whatever it takes to help Shelly."

"Me too," Kiki agreed.

Shelly smiled. She had the best mer-friends in the ocean! "Well, if you guys keep your eyes open, I will too! Now let's do this!"

The mergirls swam out of the hotel doors.

A few minutes later, they were floating in front of the temple. "Now what?" Shelly whispered to Pearl.

"Why are you whispering?" Pearl asked.

Shelly shrugged. "I don't know. Aren't curses secret or something?"

Echo shivered. "Let's just bubble down

and do this. It's sort of exciting to see the temple up close with my eyes open, but this place still gives me the creeps."

"Breaking the curse is as easy as swimming," Pearl explained. "We just have to go inside and lay these objects on the floor. Then we each need to thump our tails on the ground three times, turn around three times, and—"

"And what?" Kiki asked.

"And cross our tails with our eyes closed," Pearl finished, "while saying 'Curse of Atlas be gone.'"

"Ooh!" Echo squealed the moment they swam inside the temple. "It's so beautiful!"

"Shhh," Pearl hissed. "We're not really supposed to be in here."

Shelly gulped. What if someone kicked them out before they broke the curse? "Let's hurry," she whispered.

Pearl quickly spread out Shelly's smelly shirt with the fish, crab, bamboo, and shark's tooth. The mergirls tapped their tails three times, turned around three times, and crossed their tails. "Okay, close your eyes and say it," Pearl told them.

"Curse of Atlas be gone!" they shouted.

Shelly felt better until she heard Leslie Levee say, "What are you mergirls doing here? Tours are over for the day!" The merlady stood beside them, her hands on her hips and a frown on her face.

"Oh no," Echo gasped. "We're in trouble now!"

Pearl snatched up the shirt with the fish, crab, bamboo, and shark's tooth. "Swim for it!" she shouted.

11

AquaDome

THAT WAS SO SCARY, I almost fainted," Echo told her merfriends when they were safely back in their hotel room.

"It wasn't too bad," Kiki said.

"We're lucky Leslie didn't chase us," Pearl admitted. "We made it just in time to get ready for the championship banquet."

Moving like black marlins, the mer-girls dressed up and swam next door to the AquaDome, where the lavish dinner was taking place.

Every team in the playoffs, as well as their coaches, managers, and gymnastics teams, was already sitting at long tables. Fabulous food covered every tabletop, and delicious smells floated in the water.

But Shelly wasn't hungry. She pushed her piece of cookiecutter shark around on her shell plate and barely noticed the huge silver bowl of stalked jellyfish with blue buttons sauce on the table. "Do you think the cure will work?" she whispered to her merfriends.

"It already has," Pearl said matter-of-factly. "Nothing bad has happened since, has it?"

Shelly thought for a minute before breaking into a huge smile. "You're right!" She hugged Pearl. Shelly felt relieved. She was so glad she had told her friends. They had worked as a team, and together they had reversed the curse!

"Oh my Neptune," Pearl said. "Enough mushy stuff! Eat! You have a big game tomorrow."

Kiki passed Shelly a platter. "Try some of these oyster-thief pastries. I've heard they're delicious."

Shelly took a fluffy pastry and passed the rest on to Pearl. "I'm excited about

the games now," Shelly told her mer-
friends.

"I have a feeling the entire team is going
to do a shell-tacular job," Pearl said, grabbing a big pastry.

"Merladies and mergentlemen, may I
have your attention, please?" a burly merman announced from a podium at the
front of the room.

"That's the director of the Shell Wars
Championship Games," Kiki whispered.

The merman continued, "My name is
John Veron, and I'd like to welcome you all
to the ten-thousand-seven-hundred-and-
eighty-ninth Shell Wars Championship
Games. I am excited for the tournament
to begin tomorrow! Each of you is here

tonight because you're a star player, and you should be proud to be representing your merschools. More than that, you play as part of a team. And teamwork makes the dream work!"

Everyone in the large room clapped, stomped their fins, and cheered. Shelly felt thrilled to be part of such a wonderful tradition. Mr. Veron went on to explain how the championship playoffs work. The next morning would be filled with short elimination games, and the winners of those would play in the afternoon. The final winners would play in the evening.

Now that the curse was gone, Shelly couldn't wait for the games to begin!

The Championship Game

BY THE FOLLOWING AFTER-
noon, Shelly was exhausted.
The first game of the day
had been easy, but the second had been
rough as barnacles. Trident Academy had
made it to the final championship round,
but the team they were playing against,

the Atlantis Viperfish, were the toughest opponent they'd ever faced.

By the halftime show, Shelly could barely shake her tail. Luckily, the Rays sang a fin-tastic song about being champions. With new energy, she soared back onto the kelp field as fast as a sailfish.

The next thing Shelly knew, it was down to the game's final few merminutes, and the score was tied. Coach Barnacle called a time-out. Shelly and her fellow players huddled on the sideline.

"I'm proud of you all," Coach Barnacle said. "You've played your best, and that's all any coach can ask. For the final plays, we'll do the flea-flicker followed by the squid toss."

Shelly gulped. Usually at the end of the game, Rocky would toss the shell to Adam or another player, who would zoom toward the goal. But for the flea-flicker, Adam would give it back to Rocky, who would fling it to Shelly. Then Shelly would swim like her tail was on fire and try to score before the other team even knew where the shell was. It was a special move they had practiced only a few times.

Coach Barnacle patted Shelly on the shoulder. "You can do this," he told her. But Shelly wasn't so sure. Could she really score when it counted the most?

Shelly looked toward the side of the field. Echo, Pearl, and the rest of the Tail

Flippers were cheering "Go Trident Academy Tiger Sharks!"

Then Shelly saw Pearl wave to her, and yell, "Go Shelly!"

Shelly took a deep gulp of water. Thankfully the curse had been broken. She knew she could do this! She got in formation, and when Rocky shouted the signal "Barracuda," she was ready.

The shell zipped back and forth between Rocky and Adam, then came soaring to her. She snagged it with her stick and swam like a great white shark was chasing her. As soon as she was close to the treasure chest, she flung the shell with her stick. It whistled through the water as the Atlantis goalie reached for it.

Shelly couldn't believe what happened next.

The shell went into the chest!

"Score!" the announcer yelled just as the conch sounded to end the game. "Trident Academy wins!"

Rocky, Adam, Shelly, and the rest of the team floated for a mersecond in shock. Then Rocky grinned and yelled, "Fin-tastic!"

Suddenly John Vernon stood on the field with the golden trophy in his hands. "Merladies and mergentlemen," he announced, "it is my great pleasure to present this trophy to the Trident Academy Tiger Sharks. And congratulations to all our teams for a championship well played!"

Coach Barnacle took the trophy and lifted it high into the water. It was like a signal for the celebration to begin. Trident Academy fans soared onto the field like a shoal of herring. Everyone cheered, and Shelly saw Sarah SeaLion dump kelp juice onto Coach Barnacle's head.

The Tail Flippers flipped out onto the field. Echo and Pearl surrounded Shelly, and Kiki swam over from the sidelines. "Congratulations!" she shrieked.

"That last play scared the seaweed out of me," Echo said over the roar of the crowd. "Weren't you terrified?"

"I didn't have much time to be afraid," Shelly admitted, "but I was really grateful to Pearl for breaking the curse. We wouldn't have won if she hadn't!"

Pearl smiled. "Except that there wasn't a curse," she said.

"What are you talking about?" Shelly asked.

"I made up the cure," Pearl told them.

"All of that stuff we did was fake. There was no magazine article!"

"But—but it worked!" Shelly sputtered.

Pearl winked and said, "Yes, it did, didn't it?"

Shelly shook her head. "I don't understand. You tricked me?"

Pearl patted Shelly on the shoulder. "I did it so you'd believe in yourself. You couldn't play well if you were worried about a curse. So I had to show you that there wasn't one!"

"I can't believe the curse wasn't real!" Echo said.

Pearl shrugged. "Does it matter? We won! Go Trident Academy Tiger Sharks!"

"That was really sweet of you," Kiki told Pearl. "I had a feeling that the curse wasn't real, but I didn't know how to prove it."

Shelly shook her head. She didn't know whether she should be mad or grateful. Then she heard the crowd cheering for her team and said, "You know what I think, Pearl? I think I have the best mer-friends ever, and that makes me a winner every day!"

Journal Writing

Shelly Siren

Dear Journal,

We won! It doesn't seem real. Of course, I didn't think it would happen after I saw a spookfish in the temple. There is a legend that if you see one, you are cursed! Luckily, Pearl knew a cure for the curse. At least I thought she did. It turns out she made up everything! Now I guess I'm not cursed, because there is no such thing. At least I hope not!

Echo Reef

Dear Journal,

This has been a crazy adventure. I loved seeing all the buildings that humans built in Atlantis. I am mad at myself for keeping my eyes closed when we visited the temple. I was afraid of the curse, but it turns out there wasn't a curse at all. I could have seen all the fabulous things inside the temple for myself. But I did get to see a little bit of the entrance. I hope I get a chance to come back to Atlantis. Maybe our Shell Wars team will win again next year!

Rocky Ridge

Dear Journal,

I can't believe Coach Barnacle is making us write down our thoughts about the Shell Wars Championship. How silly is that? Anyway, I can tell you how I feel in  just a few words: Wave-tastic! Fin-tastic! Mer-velous! Shell-tacular! Splashing good! Tail-kicking!!

Kiki Coral

Dear Journal,

I'm so happy I was the Trident Academy Tiger Sharks' team manager for the Shell

Wars tournament. I didn't know it would be so much work. Managers are important. They have to make sure all the equipment is in good shape. They have to make sure everyone knows when the games are. They go to meetings and schedule practices. But most important, a team manager has to cheer for their team. Go Trident Academy!

Pearl Swamp

Dear Journal,

Atlantis is tails down the most fabulous fashion city in the ocean. I think it's better than New Ocean City. Instead of writing this, I should be shopping! I saw the cutest top in this little shop that is owned by Tyra Baybanks! Can you believe it? She is only the most famous mermodel ever! I almost fainted at the final Shell Wars game. One of the cutest princes in the whole ocean was watching: Will of the small province of Whales! Will and his wife, Kate, were sitting right beside Angelfish Molie, who I just happen to know. So when I waved, they all waved back! I can't wait to tell my friend Wanda. She is going to just die!

The Mermaid Tales Song

REFRAIN:

Let the water roar

Deep down we're swimming along

Twirling, swirling, singing the mermaid song.

VERSE 1:

Shelly flips her tail

Racing, diving, chasing a whale

Twirling, swirling, singing the mermaid song.

★ 82 ★

VERSE 2:

Pearl likes to shine

Oh my Neptune, she looks so fine

Twirling, swirling, singing the mermaid song.

VERSE 3:

Shining Echo flips her tail

Backward and forward without fail

Twirling, swirling, singing the mermaid song.

VERSE 4:

Amazing Kiki

Far from home and floating so free

Twirling, swirling, singing the mermaid song.

Author's Note

WHENEVER I WRITE A story, I always end up doing research. With the Mermaid Tales books, I get to learn about all kinds of sea creatures. But with this story, I also got to learn about sports superstitions. For instance, many people thought the Boston Red Sox baseball team was cursed after they traded away a player named Babe Ruth. For eighty-six years they didn't win the World Series. It was called the Curse of the Bambino (Babe Ruth's nickname).

Some Chicago Cubs fans wonder if Billy Sianis cursed their team when he was thrown out of a game along with his pet goat. It's called the Curse of the Billy Goat, and some fans even brought goats onto the baseball field to try to reverse the curse. Luckily, the Chicago Cubs won the World Series in 2016 and the curse is over (if there ever was one)!

People have done all sorts of things to keep away bad luck. Some good-luck charms have been horseshoes, triangles, bamboo, and wearing the same dirty socks or clothes every game. Fans of the Detroit Red Wings hockey team even believe an octopus will bring them good luck! Do you believe in good-luck charms? Or are you like Pearl, who believes you must make your own luck by believing in yourself?

Your mermaid friend,
Debbie

Glossary

ANGELFISH: This thin, colorful fish lives around reefs and eats many things, including sponges.

BARNACLE: Adult barnacles spend their lives attached to rocks, ships, or even whales.

BARRACUDA: The great barracuda is a very fast fish. Adults usually swim alone, but the young often stay together in groups called shoals.

BLACK MARLIN: Black marlins like warm water and can swim at eighty miles per hour, which is faster than cars travel on most highways.

BLUE BUTTONS: If you see what you think is a piece of blue plastic floating on the ocean's surface, it just might be a group of this unusual creature. The circular center that keeps it afloat is surrounded by stinging tentacles. Luckily, the sting isn't too powerful.

CARNATION CORAL: This colorful reef animal can be pink, red, orange, yellow, or white.

COCKLE: The common edible cockle has a ribbed shell and lives on the ocean floor.

CONCH: Large-size sea snails and their shells are called conchs. The beautiful shells come to a point at both ends.

COOKIECUTTER SHARK: This shark has a glowing green belly that attracts other fish. It also has razor-sharp teeth to take a cookiecutter-size bite out of them!

CUTTLEFISH: There are one hundred twenty different kinds of cuttlefish. The largest is the Australian Giant Cuttle-fish, but it is still only slightly bigger than a person's head.

DECOMPRESSION SICKNESS: Divers must be careful not to go too deep in the water too quickly. Diving that fast can give them this sickness.

FLAG FISH: This type of pupfish is found in Florida. It's sometimes called the Ameri-can flag fish because of the red and blue stripes on its body.

GREAT SCALLOP: The great scallop is also known as the king scallop. It can move quickly through the water by clapping the two parts of its shell together.

HERRING: Atlantic herring live in large groups, or shoals, and come to the surface at night to eat plankton.

HORSESHOE CRAB: The horseshoe crab is a close relative of spiders.

JOHN VERON: This Australian man, also known as Charlie Veron, has been nicknamed the "King of Coral" for his extensive studies of coral reefs all over the world. He is not really a merman.

KELP: Kelp is a large brown seaweed that grows in underwater forests.

LEVEE: A levee is a raised bank of dirt that is used to hold back water.

MANTA RAY: Manta rays can weigh more than a car and be wider than most people are tall.

OCTOPUS: The common octopus is an expert in camouflage. It can almost instantly change its skin color to match its surroundings.

OYSTER THIEF: This seaweed likes to live on oyster shells. As the oyster thief grows, it fills with gas and sometimes lifts itself and the oyster off the seafloor. Then the tide will carry both the oyster thief and the oyster away.

PASSION FLOWER: The passion flower is a feather star with about twenty arms. It looks like a flower and likes to live in reefs and bays.

SEA BAMBOO: Sea bamboo is the largest of the African west coast kelps. It can grow as tall as a five-story building.

SEA LION: The California sea lion is a favorite performer in marine aquariums. Sea lions eat fish and squid.

SEAWEED: There are thousands of different types of seaweed. Velvet horn seaweed is covered with fine short hairs that make it look fuzzy.

SHARPNOSE SEVENGILL SHARK: This rarely seen shark has a pointed snout and lives in deep water.

SPONGE: The Mediterranean bath sponge grows as a round gray cushion and used to be captured for use as a kitchen sponge for humans.

SPOOKFISH: This deep-sea fish is also known as a barreleye because of its unusual barrel-shaped eyes.

SQUID: The common squid is tubelike with large eyes. It can get about as long as your arm.

STALKED JELLYFISH: While most jellyfish float freely in the water, the stalked jellyfish likes to attach itself to a stalk of seaweed or sea grass.

STEAM VENT: Hot water comes from holes or vents in the earth. You may recognize them on land as hot springs or geysers. Sometimes the underwater vents cause growths called black or white smokers.

TAWNY NURSE SHARK: The tawny nurse shark is often photographed because it is usually very peaceful. But it will bite if someone threatens it!

TIGER SHARKS: Young tiger sharks have dark stripes that fade as they get older.

TRIANGULAR BUTTERFLY FISH: This triangular-shaped fish often swims in pairs and eats Christmas-tree worms (worms that live on coral and are shaped like a Christmas tree).

VENUS COMB: This snail looks surprisingly like a human comb.

VIPERFISH: This deepwater fish has huge barbed teeth and a tiny forked tail.

WATER FLEA: For such a teeny, tiny creature, the water flea has a very large eye. The water flea's body isn't even as long as a human eyelash!

Debbie Dadey

is the author and coauthor of more than one hundred and sixty children's books, including the series The Adventures of the Bailey School Kids. A former teacher and librarian, Debbie and her family live in Sevierville, Tennessee. She hopes you'll visit www.debbiedadey.com for lots of mermaid fun.

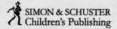

Candy Fairies

Chocolate Dreams

Rainbow Swirl

Caramel Moon

Cool Mint

Magic Hearts

Gooey Goblins

The Sugar Ball

A Valentine's Surprise

Bubble Gum Rescue

Double Dip

Jelly Bean Jumble

The Chocolate Rose

A Royal Wedding

Marshmallow Mystery

Frozen Treats

The Sugar Cup

Sweet Secrets

Taffy Trouble

The Coconut Clue

Rock Candy Treasure

A Minty Mess

Visit candyfairies.com for games, recipes, and more!